Little Gnome Tenderroot

Little Gnome Tenderroot

by

Jakob Streit

Translated by Nina Kuettel

Illustrations by Georges Feldmann

Waldorf
PUBLICATIONS

Printed with support from the Waldorf Curriculum Fund

Published by:
Waldorf Publications
Research Institute for Waldorf Education
38 Main Street
Chatham, NY 12037

Title: *Little Gnome Tenderroot*
Author: Jakob Streit
Editor: David Mitchell
Translator: Nina Kuettel
Illustrator: Georges Feldmann
German Publisher: Urachhaus, 1989
German ISBN # 978-38786-21-6
Copy Editor and Proofreader: Ann Erwin
Cover: David Mitchell
© 2010 by AWSNA
ISBN # 978-1-936367-06-1
Printed by McNaughton & Gunn
Saline, MI 48176 USA
November 2010
Reprinted 2014

Contents

Little Gnome Tenderroot and the Tree Spirit

Outside in the world it was beginning to be autumn. Some leaves on the trees were turning yellow,others red and brown. Little Gnome Tenderroot crawled out from under the Earth. He saw the first falling leaf. The wind cheerfully blew it up and down. Little Gnome Tenderroot ran after it, and he caught the leaf before it fell to the ground. He ran his hand carefully over it and was a little sad: "Little leaf will die!" he whispered.

The tree spirit peered out of the tree trunk and smiled: "What is that face you are making? Your nose is even crooked! It is better if you go down into the ground with the roots. There is a lot of life power rippling downward when the leaves decay. You can gather it in the Earth for the coming spring so that new leaves will bud. That is more important than crying over the old ones!"

"Is it flowing inside you, too?" asked Little Gnome Tenderroot. "Is that tree milk? Can you milk the roots?"

The tree spirit laughed so that its branches bounced, and he replied: "Call it what you will! I call it life power because when it drips down for a long time I become weaker and weaker. All the leaves fall down, and I sink into my winter sleep."

Tenderroot asked: "Then do you fall out of the tree?"

"No," the tree spirit giggled again. "I shrink down into the roots and become small, almost as small as you. Then I let the world be the world until the spring wakes me up again. Then I need new life power. You gnomes keep it in the Earth over the winter, and then you have to put it back into the roots in the spring. Go now, little fellow! Look! Already another leaf has fallen from me."

Tenderroot wondered if he should run after the second leaf, but the tree spirit gave him such a stern glare that he quickly turned to the left and sank back into the Earth. Down among

the roots he saw a gnome brother already plucking at them.
So, he also searched out a nice root for himself. He began
to very gently stroke the root from the top to the bottom. A
tiny glimmer appeared at the root tip, a little reddish, a little
yellowish, like sunshine. Yes, it was like milk from the sky. Little
Gnome Tenderroot thought: *If I am very good about milking,
then the leaves up there will fall and fly cheerily in the breeze.* He
was glad. The sky milk formed a little pool on the ground and
soaked into the Earth.

Little Gnome Tenderroot and the Fairies

A cold wind blew through the forest. On this day Tenderroot had milked down a lot of life power from a big oak tree. He thought: *Now I will climb up and have a look at my tree.* He turned to the right and climbed to the top. Whew! A great big bunch of brown leaves was just falling! He snatched a few out of the air and laid them under the tree next to a thick root.

But what was this? In the sky above, the good moon was shining, and a ring of fairies was dancing in the moonbeams. Gnome Tenderroot listened to their soft singing. The fairies floated so lightly up and down. They made Tenderroot feel like a heavy klutz who tramped around in the earth. He raised his arms in the air and cried: "Hey, fairies, can you take me with you? I would like to dance in a circle just once!"

The fairies giggled and snickered, came closer, swirled their veils around Tenderroot's face, tapped his little cap and his hands, and gently pulled his gnome beard. Tenderroot became quite dizzy. He sank down onto the little pile of leaves he had placed under the tree. Whether he wanted to or not, he fell asleep. While he was lying there so still, more and more fairies came down to marvel at him. They whispered:

> How still he is, and oh so sweet,
> Look at his hands and his little feet!
> He's such a little sleepyhead,
> Just like a child upon his bed.

The fairies made signs with their hands over the sleeping gnome and sang:

> Let him come and play with us,
> Lift him up, oh, what a hoot.
> Stars and moon, oh yes, we must
> Show them to dear Tenderroot!
> Moon is laughing, shining, gleaming,
> As are snowy mountain tops.
> Little gnome thinks he is dreaming,
> But the fairies know he's not.

Many wings and hands got to work to carry Gnome Tenderroot upward. They floated here, they floated there, they floated up and down, until he awakened. How happy was Gnome Tenderroot to be surrounded by the glow of the moon and stars!

Suddenly the moon made an earnest face and said: "Stop! Go no higher with him, or he will disappear like a wisp of fog. Take him back to the Earth; she is his mother. She gives him substance and form!"

The fairies obeyed and carried Tenderroot back down to his bed of leaves among the roots.

The wind had grown colder. All the fairies disappeared. The first snowflakes fell gently to the ground. One big flake landed on a gnome nose. Ker-choo! He woke up, looked around. Where were the fairies? The stars, the moon? They were covered by a snow cloud! Whew, what a chilly breeze. He stood up, turned to the left and sank into the Earth.

In the forest, winter had begun. Snow fell on the bird's nest. Snow fell on the rabbit's shrubs. Snow covered the pines and the last few leaves on the trees.

Farewell to the Winter World

How did Little Gnome Tenderroot know that all the leaves had been swept from the trees? How did he know that on the Earth above it was deep winter? Because not one single drop of life spark was coming out of any little root, no matter how he pulled on them.

The little gnome thought: *I want to go up and have a look at the winter world!* By the roots of the old oak tree, he turned around once to the right and climbed upward. Suddenly his little pointed cap and beard were sticking out of the deep snow. He used his hand to brush away the white stuff to the left and right. He made a little hole through which he peered out into the whiteness.

A little bird with blue and yellow feathers hopped up to him. It was a chickadee. She thought that a mole was trying to burrow out and make a mound of dirt here. Could one perhaps peck up a little seed or a stiff beetle? But then she saw the waving hand of Gnome Tenderroot.

He asked: "What are you doing here in the snow? The flakes will soon cover you up!"

Chickadee chirped: "I am looking for something to peck."

"Can't you peck the snowflakes? There are plenty!"

"Yes, a few beakfuls for my thirst, but they won't still my hunger."

"What stills your hunger?"

"I peck on the trees. I find little bark worms and seeds. Wherever the snow is not too thick on the ground, I can scrape up leaves."

Gnome Tenderroot was happy that the chickadee was talking to him so comfortably. He asked: "Why don't you go inside the Earth and sleep? Many animals do that."

The chickadee giggled: "Don't you know? I have a heart that beats very fast: *Tic, tic, tic. I want to hop and fly!*"

The chickadee hopped closer to Gnome Tenderroot. She lifted a wing and said: "Feel how it beats!" Somewhat shyly, the gnome laid his little hand on the bird's feather coat. Sure enough, her heart hammered and hammered, so fast that his little finger shook.

A rabbit sitting nearby had overheard their conversation. He hopped up, and Gnome Tenderroot called to him: "Little rabbit, don't you go to sleep? Do you also have to eat so that your heart goes tic-tac? What do you find in the snow?"

The little rabbit replied: "I have good scraping paws. I use them to scrape away the snow and find dried grass and leaves. My thick coat keeps me warm."

Gnome Tenderroot asked: "May I feel your tic-tac also?"

The rabbit hesitated a moment. But when he looked at the gnome, he liked him and trusted him, so the rabbit let the little gnome put his hand on his pelt. Tenderroot petted the fine fur. But when he touched an ear, it tickled the rabbit. Shwoop – he sprang to the side and scared the chickadee, who flew away chirping loudly. The little rabbit hopped away, too. His paws pressed deep holes in the snow.

Tenderroot looked around and listened to the quiet winter world. "No more fairies here," he said, a little sadly. And the little gnome went back underground, into the great stillness and rest of Mother Earth.

Midwinter

One day in the middle of winter, the Gnome King gathered his whole clan of gnomes. He said: "Dear gnomes, you have gathered all of the life force that flows from the roots into the Earth. Here it is kept for a new spring. Soon it will be midwinter and inside the Earth it begins to shine. Bring crystals and precious stones of all colors. When crystal light and life force shine upon each other, you will witness a wonder. Outside in the world the days are short now. The Sun almost cannot shine anymore. Prepare everything for the Earthlight festival!"

So, among the gnomes there began busy searching and hammering. Day after day, deep in the Earth, the crystal caves were arranged and prepared. The King himself showed them where to put the blue, red, and yellow crystals to form a rainbow. He said: "Once upon a time a Sun-child came from the heavens down to the Earth. When the child was grown, the Sun King took him up to himself. That event was etched into the Earth. When crystal light and life force shine into each other, they can show us this image. Above, on the Earth, people call it Christmas. They celebrate with candles and green trees."

The gnomes became very quiet. All hammering stopped. Nobody moved. All voices were silent. At midnight on the Holy Night, when the great stillness came on the Earth above, the great shining began. It began to ring in the crystal cave. In the middle a brilliant, sunny cloud shone forth – there! A small head, outstretched arms. The figure of a mother was woven in the blue light. The gnomes were amazed and looked with wide-open eyes at the light wonder.

Suddenly, as if flowing out of a well, waves of light streamed into the dark Earth. Light like the brilliant Sun was shining over the Child. The gnomes stepped back on all sides. Little Gnome Tenderroot stood a little in the background, but

he knew: *Now I can look into Heaven! It is even better than the fairy-moon dream!*

Slowly the light dimmed. Only a soft ring of light remained, in seven colors. Tenderroot thought: *Now the Sun King is wandering over the whole Earth.*

All at once the voice of the Gnome King sounded forth: "Take from the crystal light and carry it throughout the clefts and crevices. It will give the Earth strength for a new spring. The Earth is happy about the light!"

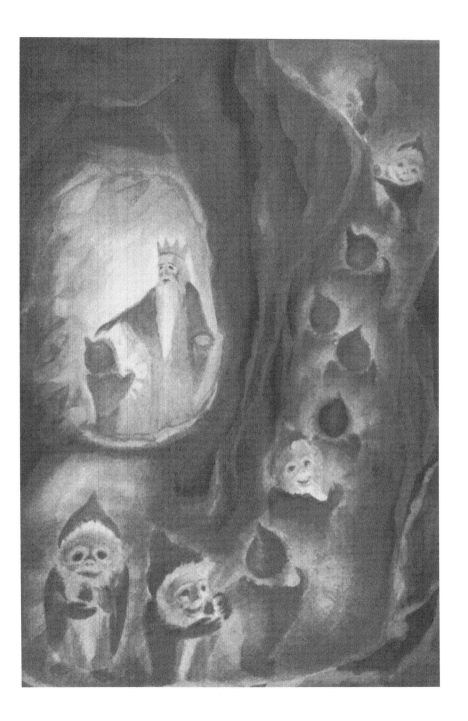

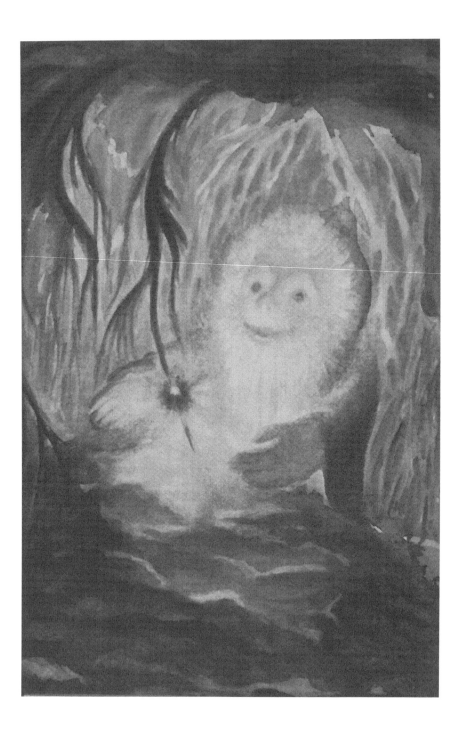

The New Year

Snow still blanketed the Earth up above when message from the King went out to all the gnomes: "Gather up life sparks in the depths of the Earth! Bring them to the slumbering seeds and roots so that spring can begin!"

As Little Gnome Tenderroot stood before the King, the King tapped his little cap: "Work hard and with cheer!" And since his spark of life light was strong, Tenderroot was allowed to join the other gnomes. They made a long, long train of light deep down in the earthy realm.

The Gnome Tenderroot looked for a nice root and breathed in its aroma. Uh, huh, bitter-sweet: "Hazelnut," he grunted. "This bush must awaken early so that it can give golden pollen to the bees." So, he put a little life spark on the root. It quietly shivered upward into the hazelnut buds and new life in the bush slowly began to show.

Tenderroot wandered around with his life sparks. He came upon a small, white bulb root. It smelled a little sour. He grunted: "Snowbell, it is time!" He stayed with the snowbells for many days until they began to jingle merrily up above.

One day Tenderroot peeked out of a little hole in the ground. The first butterflies were flying in the sunshine, and a bee crawled on a hazelnut bud. Golden pollen came out of it. Yes, look! The fairies were there again and gave him a friendly wave.

Tenderroot greeted them with his thumb – up and down, up and down, up and down. The fairies floated down to him and pulled on his little cap and beard as their way of saying hello. He gladly let them do it because he was very happy to see them again.

The Beautiful Summer Night

One summer evening Little Gnome Tenderroot was visiting the old tree spirit who knew so much about the Earth, moon, and stars. It had been a hot day. The tree spirit looked as if he were sleeping. Tenderroot tickled him on his root feet because the tree spirit loved that.

Finally, Tenderroot heard laughing from above. When he looked up, he saw the head of the tree spirit leaning out of the tree trunk, and a voice said: "Who is scratching on my leggy root?"

From below came the answer:

> It is I, Little Gnome Tenderroot!
> I want to ask, what is this all?
> The night is come and is not mute,

Everything is crawling, large and small,
And the air is filled with buzzing toots!"

The tree spirit looked up at the sky and then down again at
the roots. He began to speak:

The night is all shimmer, the Earth fairly glows,
Lightning bugs fly, and everyone knows,
Glowworms, moths, gnomes, and fairies,
The cliff-dwelling spirits in regions so airy,
Everyone will dance, be happy, and sing,
The fairies are leading their dancing ring.

Look, upon the mountain a fire burns,
People surround it as it churns.
The torrent rushes in waves of mist,
Within it the water spirits tryst.
The mountain spirit looks on in repose,
While the fairies dance with their twinkling toes.

A host of gnomes tramps in for the fun,
With lanterns to honor the season of Sun,
To thank the light of the heavenly dome,
That is the joy of every good gnome.
Golden sun gives way to silvery moon,
And the fairies dance and swirl and swoon.

Listen! People are singing:

> Summer Solstice, St. John's night,
> The loving Christ has made it bright.
> Today He blesses meadow and wood,
> And all of nature He touches with good!

Suddenly, Little Gnome Tenderroot saw a little flame dancing in front of a rock. "A will-of-the-wisp!" he called out excitedly and hurried toward it. He was so happy he wanted to snatch it with his hands, but it sprang away. Tenderroot jumped after it, and behind him hopped the whole group of gnomes:

> Hip and hop,
> Zig-zaggy, shnick-shnack,
> Hip and hop,
> Zig-zaggy, shnick-shnack!

That is what was heard, over and over. Then there was a titter and a snicker and the crickets joined in with their chirping music.

Full of curiosity, a few gloomy trolls crawled out of their holes in the ground. Their crabby faces peered out from under dark pines. They glowered around and shook their heads. They could not dance because they could not be happy. One of the trolls said: "What kind of noise is this? Foolish world!"

All at once a falling star streaked through the sky. All the gnomes called out: "Ah!" and "Oh!" But the trolls fled in alarm, back to their holes in the ground.

Tenderroot looked up at the stars for a long time, and thought: *How nice it is to be a gnome and see the wonders of the world!*

Little Gnome Tenderroot and the Dragon

Deep in the Earth, in a cave in the craggy rocks, lives a dark dragon. In the summer he sleeps. When autumn comes, he begins to yawn so that his teeth rattle and clatter. Then he begins to scratch rocky crags with his claws. He blows stinking smoke from his mouth. Michael, the angel with the sword, fought and drove him into the cave so that he keeps quiet in there. When he wakes up, being quiet is too boring for him. Then he roars, scrabbles, rumbles, and tries to break out of the cave. If a gnome mistakenly happens by, he is swallowed up and never returns.

One time, when the dragon had awakened, Gnome Tenderroot wandered very close to the cave. He was carrying some root-light in his hands because he was taking it deeper

into the Earth. All at once he heard far-away snorting and scratching.

What could that be? he thought, and he was curious. He climbed down a little way, but then the air started to stink. Through a crack in the rock he glimpsed a shimmering, greenish light. When Tenderroot looked further into the crack, he saw the dragon! He was frightened, and he dropped the blossom root-light he was holding. It fell down through the crack, dripped onto the dragon's scales and made white steam.

The dragon bellowed and hollered and blew at the light with his black breath. The cave quaked. Tenderroot climbed up as fast as he could. When he came to where the other gnomes were gathered, he told them what had happened.

The master gnome said: "You went too deep into the Earth. Since Michael defeated him, the dragon hates the light and lives in darkness. He is a swallower of light. Do not carry the light any deeper than the place where the crystals gleam. That way nothing bad will happen to you. But the more sunlight we take from the roots and give to the Earth, the weaker the dragon becomes in his dark cave."

Since that time Little Gnome Tenderroot has been careful not to go too deep into the darkness of the Earth. Instead, he stays busy gathering sunlight from the roots of the plants and giving it to the Earth.

Made in the USA
Las Vegas, NV
11 January 2021

15725899R00024